3
Magic Dreams

By
Matt Bolton Art

AuthorHouse™ UK
1663 Liberty Drive
Bloomington, IN 47403 USA
www.authorhouse.co.uk
UK TFN: 0800 0148641 (Toll Free inside the UK)
UK Local: 02036 956322 (+44 20 3695 6322 from outside the UK)

ISBN: 978-1-6655-9156-0 (sc)
978-1-6655-9157-7 (e)

Published by AuthorHouse 07/23/2021

authorHOUSE

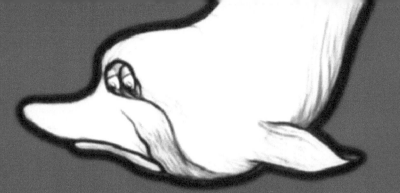

Contents

GILBY

By
Matt Bolton Art

Over the sea and far away
on a lonely island small and grey,
lived Gilby, with Simon the dinosaur,
and also a seal called Eleanor.
The dinosaur was always sad.
The seal infact was just as bad.
So he would only ever moan,
and she was so worried
she'd only groan.

All they ever had to eat was
fish that tasted of stinky feet.
This might seem sad to me and you,
but it was all they ever knew.

Then suddenly there came a day
when not one fish would come their way,
not only that day but all of the next.

They grew more and more hungry,
and more and more vexed!

Desperate, Gilby made a raft,
and bravely set out on his craft.
As he sat patiently hoping for a bite,
unbeknown to him and well out of sight.

A giant blue monster rose up from below,
to swallow poor Gilby in one single go.

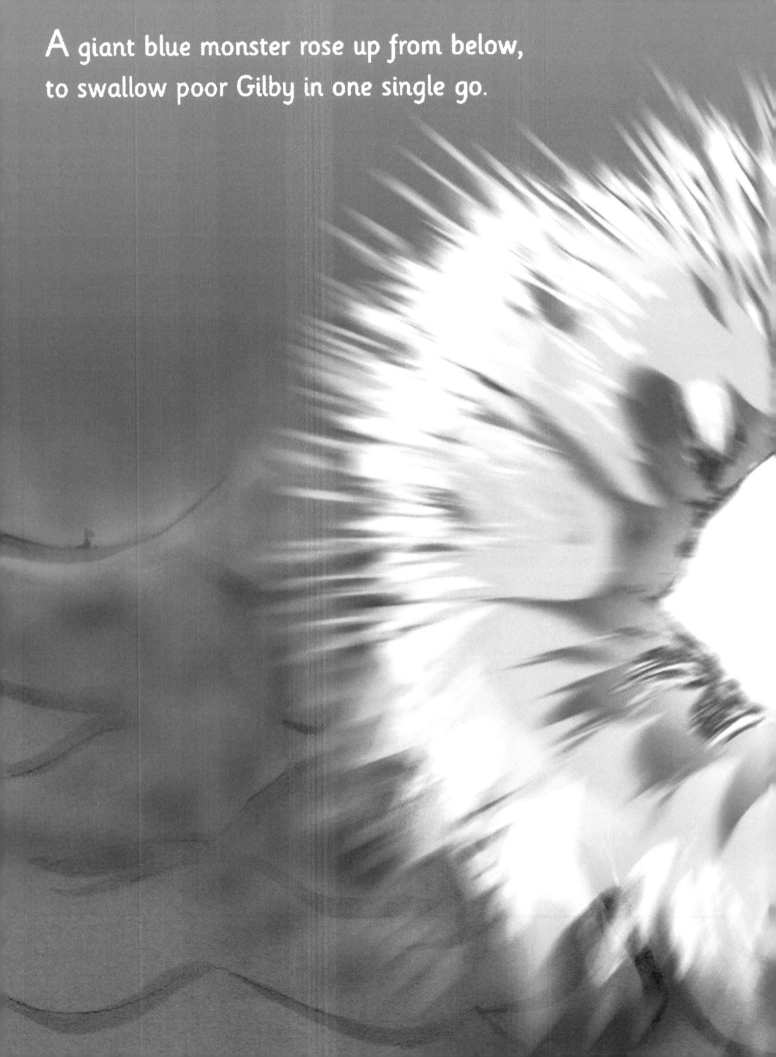

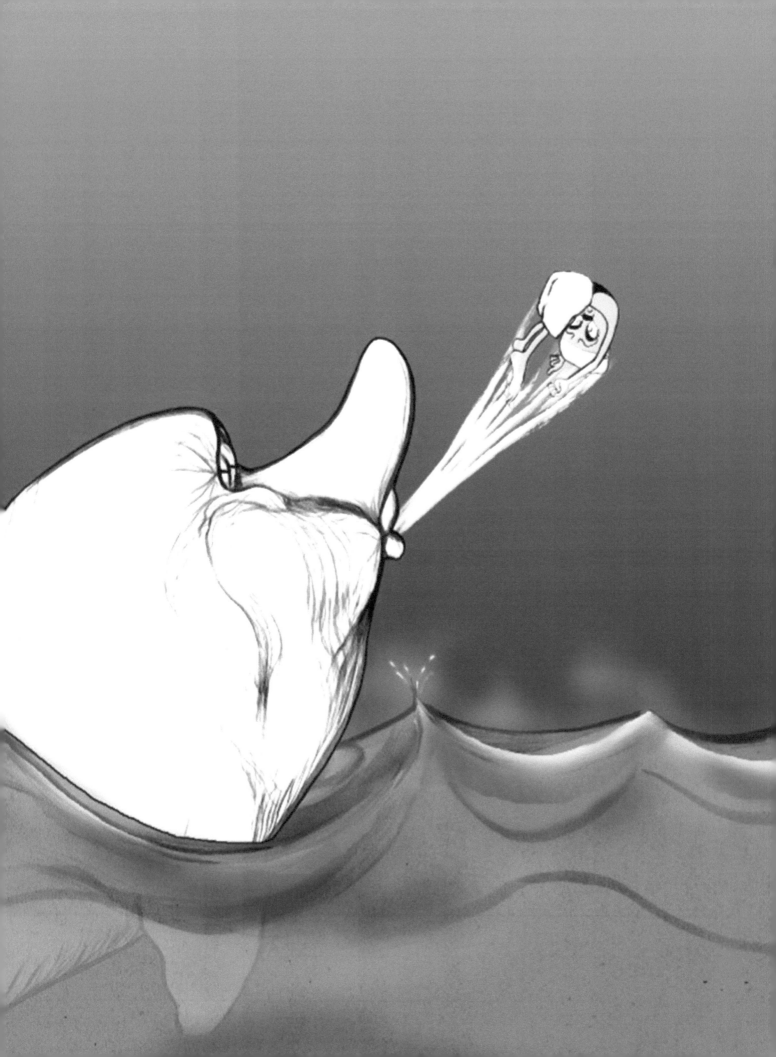

But when the beast tasted just one lick,
the taste of feet made it feel quite sick!

It spat him so far away into the sky,
stars up above were soon catching his eye.

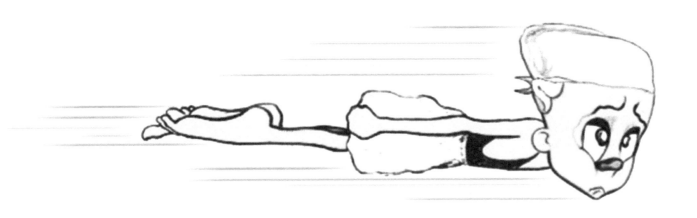

For Gilby this seemed very lucky!

The monster just though 'Oh how yucky!'

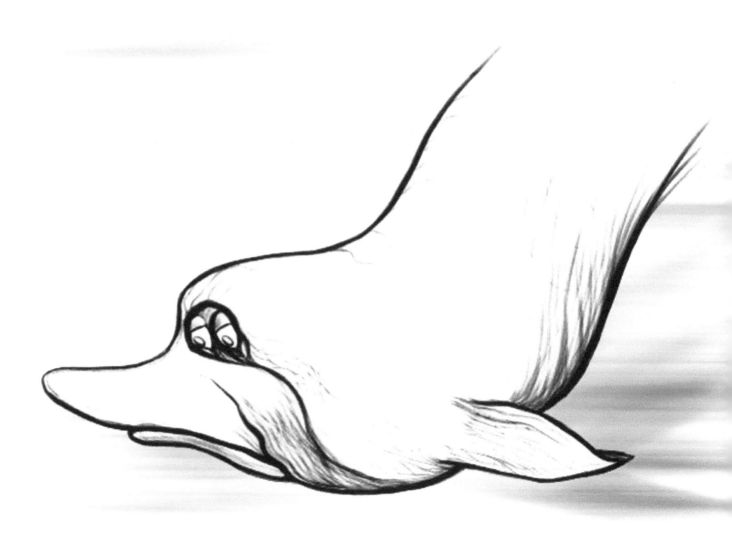

Gilby flew towards some land,
with brilliant trees and golden sand.
He thought he'd drop with a massive crash...

Luckily he landed with hardly a splash.
He fell straight onto a gigantic weed,
which did a bit more than reducing his speed.
Down he slithered from leaf to leaf
until he landed quite safely beneath.

Two strange creatures, sitting nearby
were shocked to see Gilby fall from the sky.

One said kindly "Don't be scared, but if you speak,
how did you come to fall here at our feet?
My name's Zac, I'm at your service,
and my friend is Ed,
there's no need to be nervous!"

Then Gilby told them his strange story
of hungry friends who felt so poorly,
and of the monster with the gaping jaw,
who had just spat him onto their floor.

Zac said "Hey, don't worry anymore today!
We'll make sure you're all okay.
Here eat this fruit to stop your hunger,
and have this bag full of magic wonder."

Gilby wondered what was fruit,
but soon found out the taste did suit.
It really tasted very yummy!
and soon the hunger left his tummy.

Next he asked about the magic
"It'll help to make your home less tragic.
Sprinkle it over your isle tonight,
and then just wait till morning light."

A quick goodbye and up Ed flew,
carrying Gilby and some fruit to.
Gilby carried his magic sack
in his mouth the whole way back.

They flew towards the smell of feet,
wafting stronger each wing beat.
It began to make Ed feel quite queasy,
apart from that, the trip was easy.

Ed dropped Gilby off and turned to leave,
before the smell could make him heave.
"Thank you" called Gilby, tear in eye,
at such a sudden sad goodbye.

His friends though stared with great delight
to see Gilby back from his epic flight.
Eleanor was feeling such relief
that her clapping was beyond belief!

Seeing Gilby return Simon felt such relief,
for once in a life time he forgot all his grief.
He nearly managed to smile
and show off his teeth,
but smiling takes practice
when your life has been so bleak.

The fruit was swiftly passed around,
and a liking for it was quickly found.
Savouring such a lovely taste,
they gobbled it down with urgent haste.

Then Gilby scattered far and wide,
the magic gift that Zac supplied.

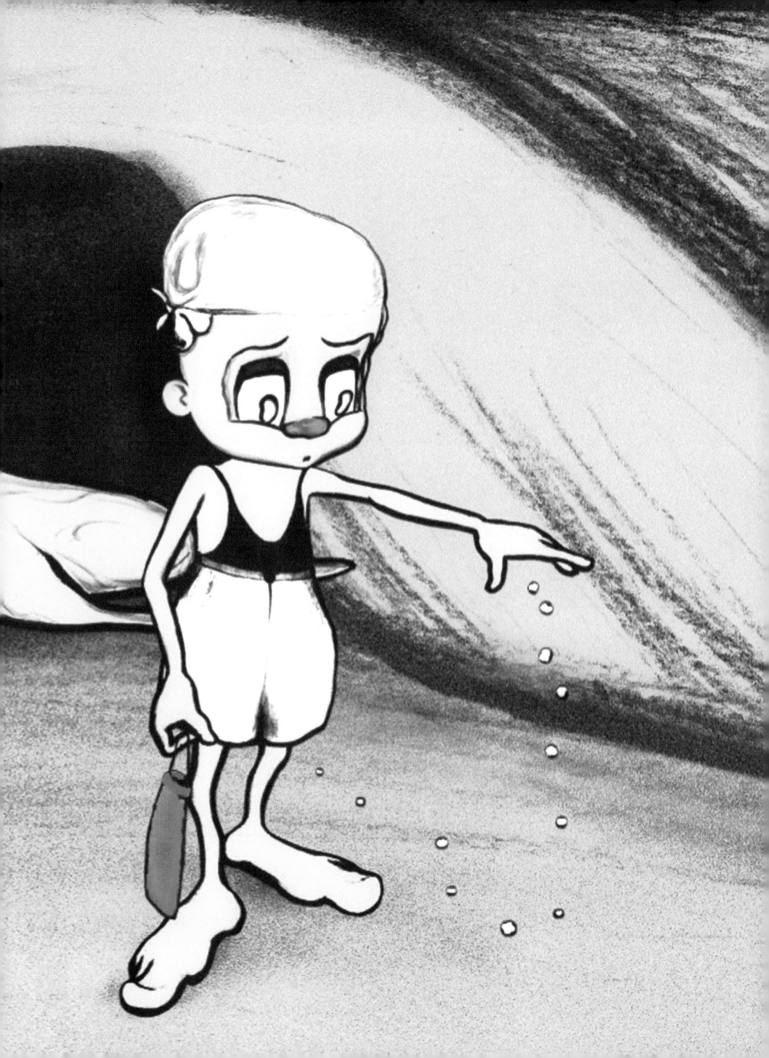

It didn't take long for change to show.
Their island got bigger,
and plants started to grow.

Not just plants but fruit as well,
all with such a fragrant smell.

There were fruits with tastes
like treacle toffee,
candy floss and milky coffee.

Their island kept growing,
bigger and bigger.
Becoming a paradise
with infinite vigour.

The island glowed with colours bright,
the once grey sky a blue delight.

Their grey skin vanished without a trace,
bringing healthy colour to each face.

Simon just beamed throughout the day,
and Eleanor cast her cares away.

Of course, best of all,
the air was sweet,
not a hint of stinky feet.

The
Time Machine
Twins

by Matt Bolton Art

The twins next birthday was drawing near.
They hoped it wouldn't be like last year.
Remote control helicopters soon lost their appeal.
Their disappointment had been hard to conceal.
After the toys had lost their lustre
They just sat in a cupboard getting dustier.

In the year 2050
Children's toys were really nifty.
But the one that had caught the twins attention
Seemed like a magical new invention.
By far the best thing the twins had seen
Was the Infinity Junior Time Machine.
It looked really great, all shiny and new
But most important was what it could do.
Travel through time and really amaze.

But their parents thought "Just another new craze.
It can't actually travel through time." they knew.
That was simply impossible to do.
Their birthday was coming and the twins were quite sure
What they wanted this year. Not like before!

When at last the day came, to their delight
The Infinity Junior Time Machine was a most welcome sight.

Their parents were really delighted
To see the twins happy and so excited.
Not for a moment did they dream
That this toy was much more than it might seem.

So they happily watched the twins jump inside
And left them to play their imaginary ride.

The twins also wondered "Could it be True"
Only one way to find out they knew.
So without stopping to read any instructions
Zac pressed a button. What an eruption!
Immediately there was buzzing and shaking,
Swirling colour's all quite breath taking.
An electronic trick or was it for real?
To travel through time would be such a big deal.

When they got out it was straight away clear

That they had definitely travelled somewhere.

It had really worked, how fantastic.

By now the twins were simply ecstatic.

Nearby was a pool surrounded by creatures
Which they had only seen in pictures.
Dinosaurs, but not big or too scary.
So Bev and Zac were not at all wary.

One of them curiously came to the pair
Sniffing and snuffling the cool clear air.
Bev gave it a sweet from a packet she found
And it gobbled it down, then sniffed around
As the others lined up hoping to eat
Some of the delicious treat.

But while they all jostled squeaking for more
They suddenly heard a fearsome roar.
The dinosaurs all scurried away
As fast as they could, not wanting to stay.

Then the reason became clear.
They saw a dinasour that didn't look so friendly.
It was a gigantic Tyranosaurus Rex,
and it was staring straight at them.

With a monstrous mouth full of sharp teeth,
it could easily snap up
a little boy or girl in one bite.

So the twins, hand in hand, ran as fast as they could
Fleeing the monster on whom sweets were no good.
Just in time they scrambled inside
And pressed a button, desperate to ride.

Again the machine buzzed and shook.
The dinosaur hadn't made it kaput.
The twins, still in shock after what they'd withstood
Climbed carefully out. It seemed quite good.

A massive construction stood nearby,
Of massive stones reaching up to the sky.
But for now they had learned to take much more care.
Maybe they could find the instructions somewhere...

Bev finally found them on an I Pad
And they sat down to read them . It was bad!

INFINITY JUNIOR TIME MACHINE.
INSTRUCTIONS:

1 Do not exit the machine in any
  time period except from 2050.

2 Always stay inside the time machine.

3 View different time periods from
  inside machine.

4 Do not exit the time machine.

5 Make sure the battery is fully charged
  before travel.

OOPS!

They looked at each other, the danger now clear
Of just rushing in without any fear.

They turned to go back inside the machine
Then saw figures advancing and looking quite mean.
They watched for a second, eyes open wide
Then jumped back behind some rocks to hide.

The figures were cavemen, and getting quite near.
They grunted and groaned, their dialect unclear.
The twins clearly needed to get away now.
But with cavemen advancing they didn't know how.

Then it was too late, because they had seen
The Infinity Junior Time Machine.
Wow! They circled around it transfixed
Pointing and grunting, seeming bewitched.

The twins stayed hidden and watched hardly breathing
Amazed by all the things they were seeing.

And then the cavemen knelt down and low
And bent forwards in a worshipful row.

They started to hum and then to sing
Bowing to the machine in an awesome ring.

The singing continued as it grew night
And a beautiful moon filled the sky with light.

Then the cavemen started to dance
All the while in a mystic trance.
They jumped and gyrated round and round
Clapping and stamping. The twins were spellbound.

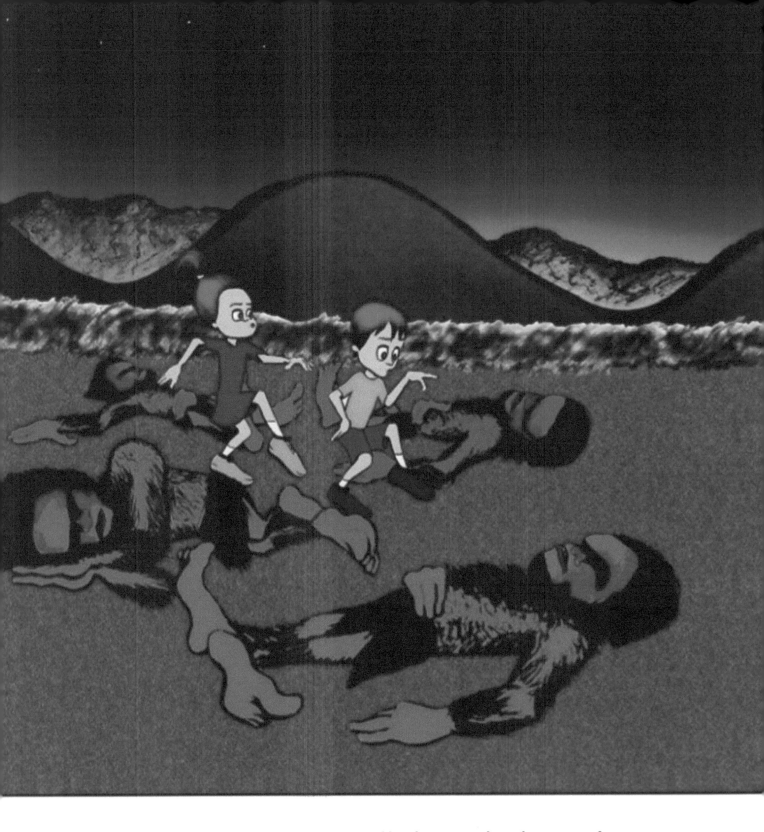

The twins watched on all through the night.
'Till the cavemen collapsed in dawn's coming light.
Exhausted they could dance no more.
They fell fast asleep stretched out on the floor.

Now was their chance so the twins tiptoed past
Free to return to the machine at last.

This time they took great care, not just guessing

Which of the buttons they should be pressing

"We'd better not say all the things we have seen

Travelling in our time machine.

They'll never allow us to use it again

And that would be tragic, a terrible pain."

Dara's Dreams

By
Matt Bolton Art

Dara lives with his family,

Mum and Dad and the cat makes three.

While Dara likes to play with his toys

What the others do best is make lots of noise.

Lots of noise, noise, noise noise!

Sometimes laying awake at night

Becuase of the noises, he thought there might

Be fantastic creatures flying by

Far above in the evening sky.

In the deep dark night when you're in your bed

You never can tell what's overhead.

A gigantic eagle as big as a plane.

Nobody knows what the skies contain.

There are many mysteries unresolved,

And unknown creatures may well have evolved.

Like flying sharks with special powers

For hunting in the long night hours.

Enormous flies all with colourful wings.

Scary bugs amongst other things.

Have you ever wondered why we dream?
Those strange night time stories that often seem
To pop into your head quite uninvited
Making you sometimes scared and sometimes delighted.

In Dara's case at night in bed
Those unending sounds flowed into his head
Firing up his imagination
Creating dreams full of fascination.

Somewhere near a phone was ringing.
That turned into beautiful birds sweetly singing

And Dad's monotonous telephone chatter
Became mischievous monkey natter,

Which startled the birds and made them fly
Far away up into the sky.

Then a noisy flush in the bathroom sounded
Like rushing water in which his bed floundered.
A fearsome flood swept Dara away.

But it was his bed which saved the day
For on the wild wave Dara surfed high
Feeling almost as if he could fly.

Later that night a visitor crept
Onto his bed as Dara slept.
His little cat with a very loud purr
Snuggled beside him with soft silky fur.

Dara lay dreaming of a far away land.
There were rocket topped pyramids, and
A loveable lion who just wanted to play,
So the two stayed together all the long day.

Sitting astride the lions strong back
For a ride on a long and winding track
Through that strange purple world, they went
Happy together and quite content.

Having a lion for a pet.
How much better could it get?
Much more fun than a little cat.
Dara gave the lion a pat,
Hoping they would never part.
Blissfully happy until with a start.....

The lion let out an almighty roar.
Which terrified Dara to the core.
"Oh no" he thought, "this lion might
Gobble me up with just one bite."

Then Dara woke up with a start,

Trembling and with a racing heart.

The roaring still rang in his ears

But he quickly put aside his fears.

Mum was outside in dawns early glow
Giving the lawn yet another mow.

Her monstrous mower with its rattle and roar
Made all the neighbours dread any more.

Lightning Source UK Ltd.
Milton Keynes UK
UKHW050500231021
392696UK00002B/59